George J. Holyoake

The Path I took, and where it Led Me

An Autobiography and Argument

George J. Holyoake

The Path I took, and where it Led Me
An Autobiography and Argument

ISBN/EAN: 9783337119379

Printed in Europe, USA, Canada, Australia, Japan

Cover: Foto ©Raphael Reischuk / pixelio.de

More available books at **www.hansebooks.com**

THE PATH I TOOK,

AND

WHERE IT LED ME.

An Autobiography and Argument.

BY

A MONMOUTHSHIRE FARMER.

REVISED BY G. J. HOLYOAKE.

PRICE SIXPENCE.

LONDON:

WATTS & CO., 17, JOHNSON'S COURT, FLEET ST., E.C.

BRISTOL:

G. W. HARVEY, 7 AND 8, LOWER ARCADE.

DEDICATION.

REMARKS BY THE REVISER.

On reading the MS. of this pamphlet, it appeared to me worthy of publication—for its passages of curious experience, its shrewdness of argument, and the moral vigour of its social advice to young people as well as to farmers. I have made no addition to it—it required none. I have changed nothing, for that would have impaired the originality of the story. In some places I found repetitions, and now and then prolixity such as any writer having fervour in his pen might fall into. Here I have made abridgments, which is all I have done.

G. J. HOLYOAKE.

THE PATH I TOOK, AND WHERE IT LED ME.

Born on December 25th, 1814, I have had the privilege of living through the greater part of this most eventful century, and have had therefore considerable opportunity of observing the important progressive changes that have taken place during this long period.

My father and his family were Church people of the formal and conventional type, whilst my mother was a descendant of a long line of Congregationalists, of whose Church she was an earnest member. My father died when I was eight years old, leaving my mother with four children, one son and three daughters, to rear and educate, which she did after a very motherly fashion; and her widowhood extended for the long period of thirty-eight years. Our school education in those days was scant and inferior in quality. I got so far as to read and spell fairly well, and to write a very indifferent hand. Part of this instruction I obtained in a Church Sunday-school, so had an early opportunity of being informed as to the theories, doctrines, ceremonies, observances, and practices connected with the Church of England, which, I may here add, failed as time went on to yield me satisfaction. My connection with the Church continued for several years; first as a scholar, and then as a member of the church choir. But my first serious difficulty with, and estrangement from, the Church arose from my observation of the inconsistent, unseemly, and, I may add, flagrantly immoral conduct of the clergy of my acquaintance, which for several reasons I cannot pass over in silence.

The vicar of our parish, about the years 1822-3, had decamped to France in debt, whilst he was living in idleness on the tithes derived from the labours of the farmers of our parish and the adjoining one. He therefore com-

mitted the cure of souls (so-called) to the custody of a
clergyman whose only qualification for the office was his
great physical ability for the performance of an incredible amount of work upon the day of rest, proving the
truth of the apostle's assertion that religion is profitable
for this life.   His Sundays were days of special activity.
I have known him for a considerable time perform
four Church services on a Sunday, catechise the children
at one of the churches, and travel twelve miles of bad
road to accomplish this heavy task.   Such was his
great love for souls.   But then he had the whole week to
recruit his strength by pipe and glass.   On Sunday, when
on the point of going into church, he would jocularly say
to the landlord of the inn : "Let us have another glass,
Tommy, and then I'll preach till the devil comes out of
them."   What an acquisition such a man must have been
to the ministry!   How the devils must quake and tremble
on seeing him ascend the pulpit stairs!   But good as were
our parson's temporal means, he was not satisfied.   Know-
ing that the vicar was afraid to show his face to his
creditors in England, he concocted a plan to increase his
stipend by forming an alliance with a lawyer's clerk, by
whose aid he robbed the tithe-payers of the parishes
over which he was clergyman of a large sum of money
after this wise :—They gave the tithe-payers notice of a
rise in the tithe without the knowledge of the vicar,
dividing the spoil between themselves—with this exception,
that the lawyer, like the monkey in dividing the cat's
stolen cheese, monopolised the larger share, by which the
parson was sadly chagrined.   This course continued for
years, until a farmer came to live among us who appeared
better adapted for a lawyer than a farmer.   This person
managed to get the address of the vicar, and ascertained
from him that he had no knowledge whatever of any rise
in the tithe ; and through the influence of this man the
tithe was reduced to its former rate.   These transactions
occurred about the years 1824-5-6.   Being of a somewhat
sensitive turn of mind, I began early to contemplate my
position as regards religion.   God as represented to me
appeared to be an almighty, austere, and revengeful being
whom I was instructed to love with all my heart, mind,
soul, and strength.   I seemed to be suspended or oscil-
lating between heaven and hell, without any assurance of

escaping the miseries of the one, or attaining the bless-ings of the other state of existence. About the year 1828 a young man came to live with us as farm-bailiff. As a religious man he was a person of extraordinary character. He attended church with the greatest punctuality, was very conscientious and devotedly religious, and, as a matter of course, a regular communicant. On a certain Whit-Sunday he had received the sacrament at the hands of our parson, and the next day, Whit-Monday, as he passed along the highway he met his pastor on horseback in such an intoxicated condition that he could with difficulty retain his seat. This incident proved a great shock to the pious young man. But this was not the worst, for he soon discovered that his pastor was not an occasional, but an habitual drunkard. This induced him to throw overboard the Church for ever ; and he became a member of the Baptist persuasion, of which denomina-tion he was a most zealous and consistent member to the end of his life. Although I failed to agree with him as to his religious convictions, I ever respected him for his sincerity and endeavour to be consistent with his profes-sion. But with regard to this clergyman, the tale I have to unfold reflects considerably upon his character as a Christian teacher, or an exemplar of morals. He had a most amiable wife, whom he treated with the greatest brutality when in a state of mad intoxication. She has been known to flee from him for her life in the night, with no covering but her nightdress, to the first cottage she could find, which was a considerable distance off, but she was glad to take refuge in the most humble cottage as a temporary asylum from his brutal conduct. Our clergyman was also the father of a large family, com-prising two sons and several daughters, the latter follow-ing closely in the footsteps of their mother, which pro-cured them the high esteem of all their neighbours. But they also suffered considerably in body and mind from the intemperate habits and cruelty of their father, who, having proved by practical experience what a jolly life was that of a clergyman, how easily obtained, how independent when realised, with six holidays weekly in which he could disport himself with pipe and glass, naturally asked what profession extant could he choose for his sons with advantages so great, obtained at so little cost and entailing so little responsibility ? He, as a matter of course, sent them into the Church without regard to their suitability for the office. But it is pleasant to admit that the elder one, although of a somewhat eccentric character, comported himself with greater propriety than the average clergyman does. But what shall we say of the younger one ? Well, he was a veritable chip of the old block, but had less discretion or greater ill-luck than his father, for he oftentimes got into hot water that would severely scald a sensitive man. After making his début as a Church minister, he soon fell into difficulty in this wise,—he with another clergyman of the same manner of mind lived together in the same house in which they jointly kept an housekeeper. This lady soon became embarrassed as to her bodily condition, which she attributed to the improprieties of the clergyman of my acquaintance. This he positively denied, maintaining that his friend and fellow-clergyman was the cause of the lady's trouble. The case was tried in Petty Sessions and the decision of the magistrates went against my neighbour. Not satisfied with this decision, he appealed to the Court of Quarter Sessions. But the Court confirmed the decision of the magistrates, so he had to accept its consequences, one of which was, that he was suspended from his office for two or three years, during which time, although residing in his father's house, he did not attend Church to hear him, nor any one else. But he could go a journey of twenty miles, more or less, to fill a vacancy for another clergyman when a guinea or two could be got by filling the office. Here we have substantial proof of the moral value and the religious advantages of State-supported religion.

Having thus got into the disgrace referred to, and also being a man of very intemperate habits, of which I have personally been cognizant, one would naturally suppose that his mode of life would render him ineligible ever afterwards to fill the office of a Christian minister. But not so ; Mother Church looks with remarkable leniency upon the lapses of her wayward children, such as were unmistakably exemplified in the case of the person under notice. For in the course of time the living of the two parishes of which his father had been curate for the long period of fifty years became vacant, and he (the son) was duly inducted into it. By this means his circumstances were materially improved, but without producing any improvement in his moral character; but contrariwise, he went from bad to worse. He again fell into trouble with one of his female domestic servants, but he managed to avoid any great publicity, or the intervention of the Bishop of the diocese—by submitting to an agreement as to pecuniary compensation. But the looseness and self-indulgence of his life told early upon his constitution, though it was by no means delicate. In the course, therefore, of a few years he became paralysed, body and mind, giving way so far that he was obliged to procure substitutes to fill the office he had for years disgraced. The above reference to the conduct of these clergymen has not been dictated by any ill feeling towards them individually or their family. For I admit that notwithstanding their general unfitness to fill the office of teachers of the people as Christian ministers, they yet, as a family, possessed amiable traits of character which secured the good will of their neighbours, and prevented or suppressed the exposure of much of their conduct that was incompatible with the office of Christian ministers. It is an old saying that charity covereth a multitude of sins. And the individual destitute of all good qualities must be a *rara avis*. It is well known that men and women who indulge in the use of intoxicants to a great excess, possess oftentimes some admirable qualities that are not to be found in many a teetotaler, or temperance advocate. But this is not intended as a rebuke or reproach to the temperance movement, to which I hold society is greatly indebted.

My object is not to treat with disparagement any institution adapted (in my judgment) to elevate the moral condition of society. But I have a strong conviction, of many years' growth, that the great temptations held out by the Church of England to men of all classes and descriptions of character to enter its ministry are so great as to render the Church a source of gross corruption, not only in its ministry, but its adherents generally. For it is to-day a fact as it was thousands of years ago,—"As are the priests so are the people." If the priesthood is corrupt, the people are sure to imbibe the corruption also. You cannot associate yourself with any corrupt institution without morally suffering, more or less, from the alliance; and so convinced am I of the corrupt and corrupting

influence of the Church and its disastrous consequence to
the well-being of society (although there are many of
great amiability attached to it), that this alone has
prompted me to make these damaging revelations in accord
with my experience and observation. To this end I may
further say that the vicar just referred to, having become
incapable of filling his office, was obliged to employ substitutes. One of these followed, be it noted, closely in
the foot-steps of our vicar and his father. He displayed
the same immoral propensities, pursued the same mode of
life, and was as utterly careless of the religious condition
of the people as were his predecessors. Here were three
clergymen, following each other consecutively as ministers
in the same churches for a period considerably over half
a century. What shall we say of a religious system productive of such results, and in which men of such marked
unfitness can with ease enter its ministry and continue
therein during their lifetime? If such cases were of rare
occurrence, there would be some excuse; but the temptations held out by the Church are so strong and the advantages so great that the most unworthy and inefficient
persons are induced to seek admission into its ministry
without any apparent compunction whatever, especially
when backed by wealth and position. Such is a phase of
the religion of Jesus in this, the last, decade of the nineteenth century, as exemplified under the combined influence
of Church and State. Some years ago I was intimately
acquainted with a young man, as I have been with all
the clergymen before referred to. This young man had
no means of obtaining a living besides working, for which
he had no relish, and was consequently a hanger-on to his
friends. But it must be said that his father was a clergyman, his uncle was a clergyman, he had two cousins
clergymen. What a hardship it would have been, then,
for this young man to have remained out in the cold, and
to have to get his bread by the sweat of his brow—to
submit to the curse which they teach is the lot of man,
but which the clergy manage dexterously to avoid as it
affects themselves. So the friends of this young man,
clerical and lay, combined together to deliver him from
the consequences of the curse aforesaid, which they did
by sending him to a University. And no sooner had he
left college than he obtained a curacy of some importance

and was considered as a very promising young clergyman. He had an excellent voice, which is a sufficient recommendation for a clergyman to many people; consequently he became the pet of the snobbery of the locality, and it was asserted that his vicar worked him very hard. Poor fellow, he was anxious to escape hard work. But not only did he, as report said, work hard, but he gave much of his time and company to promote the enjoyment of convivial meetings frequently held in the place. Thus matters went on for a time in quite a festive manner, but suddenly a report, like a loud clap of thunder, rang through the locality that the curate had disappeared. Yes, he disappeared from the place for ever; never to be known there again as a public man. But the worst part of the matter was, that he left his creditors to square up matters without his intervention in the best way they possibly could. This young gentleman never put in an appearance here as a Church minister again. One would have thought that such unfavourable incidents would militate, if not prove fatal to, his success hereafter as a minister of the Christian religion. But Mother Church is not austere to her erring children, but remarkably lenient, and she looked upon this affair apparently as a foible of youth of quite a venial character, and opened her doors sufficiently wide for the reception of her delinquent son in a county and diocese where he was wholly unknown. Here report says he got married and became the father of sons whom, as a matter of course, he brought up as clergymen. This I regard as not an unfair specimen of how clergymen are manufactured for the Church of England.

We have ample proof of the worthlessness of numbers of the clergy, and their unsuitability as moral guides or pioneers in the service of the people; whereas we require the best of men—men of intellectual power and moral worth—to aid us in our attempt to discover truth among the numerous and discordant theories that are ever ringing in our ears and eminently calculated to produce confusion of thought. In the parish where I have resided for the long period of seventy to near eighty years six clergymen in succession have officiated, not one of whom has given any demonstrative proof that he had any care or anxiety whatever for what is called the spiritual condition of the people. Yet one of these clergymen I must single out as characterised by great friendliness and courtesy towards his parishioners. He would pay them weekly visits in a social and cordial manner. But he always considerately abstained from introducing religious topics into his conversation, even in the presence of the irreligious, the indifferentists, and those whose avowed convictions ran counter to his. How are we to account for this? Is it the result of faithlessness or inhumanity? Certainly not the latter. There was not one of these clergyman, it may be fairly presumed, but would render assistance in case his neighbour's life were in peril; or that would refuse to aid him in case his house were on fire. But here, in a matter which is described by the clergy in our churches as of infinite importance to each individual, even when human life is ended, we fail to recognise them endorsing these teachings in their every-day conduct, but rather ignoring and abandoning them. Such then is the faithlessness or infidelity of the clergy as exhibited by their conduct in view of their avowed profession. It would appear that we have to pay very dear for our whistle when we take into account its note. How many hundreds per year should we give to such men as I describe? The salt that has lost its savour is good for nothing, but to be cast out and trodden under the feet of men. It is a gross outrage upon Church adherents themselves to have men of low moral and intellectual capacity imposed upon them as public religious teachers whom they are legally bound to maintain through life, let their inconsistency of character and general worthlessness be ever so apparent. If this imposition is offensive to Churchmen, as it inevitably must be, what can be the feelings of Nonconformists of every creed and persuasion relative to this matter? Weak and impotent as human nature is, acts of despotism and dominancy cannot be perpetrated by one Christian section upon the others without giving rise to a spirit of virtuous indignation. Sad, indeed, would be our case, if herein we failed. We should not allow ambitious individuals, nor intolerant institutions, whatever their ancestry or antiquity, to ride rough-shod over our civil and religious liberties. Such conduct would indicate inadequate moral courage and incapacity to protect ourselves against the wiles and machinations of oppressors and despots. It is astonishing to observe how Churchmen aspiring to be lights and leaders of society (many of whom are of amiable private character) uphold with all their influence an institution of such a despotic and arbitrary character, which palpably contravenes the teachings of him whom in theory they claim as Lord and Master, and who taught his disciples to act justly towards others by doing to them only as they would wish to be done by. This command, held to be of divine authority, is enforced by a significant test affecting conduct, comprised in the following exhortation : "If ye love me keep my commandments." Yet in practice it is quite obvious that these injunctions are in religious matters virtually ignored or practically abandoned by professors of religion when opportunity and material interest require. The duty, therefore, of rescuing society from the thraldom of the Church under which it has so long been weighed down, is of no mean import.

Thus we have seen the Church of England holding for years the Irish people, who were bound in her iron grip, and compelled to be subservient to her, although avowedly an alien Church. Here we have a significant exhibition of the infidelity of the Church to the moral teaching of the scriptures. Again, with regard to Wales and Monmouthshire, her conduct has been of the same high-handed and despotic character.

In past years the Church troubled little about the condition of Wales as regards religious matters. They left these matters to the Nonconformists, whose activity and progress at length disturbed their equanimity, and became productive of serious alarm lest the emoluments monopolised by the clergy should flow into channels of a more just and equitable character. For the Church of England consisting, as it does in Wales, of a minority of the people, yet dominates over the majority, compelling them to support her by the force of Church-made laws under State influence. The signs of the times have latterly so aroused the adherents of the Church that both the clergy and laity have put forth all their energy to maintain intact the Established Church, it being the great reservoir or depository of wealth from which the clergy draw their millions per annum, wrung from the toil and industries of the people—the vast majority of whom are not attached to the Church, and many that are apparently so must be set down as coerced by the pressure of external circumstances.

Yes, money and arbitrary power are the real object, the transparent secret, the Alpha and Omega, the beginning and the end of the Church's zeal as to religion. This influence she uses with great assiduity to frustrate the political, social and moral progress of the people. The active patrons and adherents of the Church are ever the enemies of the political advancement of the people—the conservators of privilege, tyranny and oppression. Hence they belong to the Tory school. I will here recite a vivid instance of the scandalous treatment of a public official by the Tories in South Monmouthshire some years ago. The person I allude to held the office of Surveyor of the Highways, which he filled with efficiency and general satisfaction. Even his political opponents felt bound to praise him, and pronounced him a competent surveyor. Since the general change in the management of the highways, we in this district have had six surveyors, all of them respectable men. But not one of them surpassed if equalled the person in question for thorough-going competency. But this man, admirably as he filled his office, courteous and manly as was his general demeanour, nevertheless, as one of the people, naturally and consistently held Radical politics in a free and open manner, and was capable of expressing himself with considerable effectiveness, the result of natural ability. This gave great offence to the Tory magnates of the neighbourhood, who took counsel together to expel him from office, and this they succeeded in carrying out by the pressure of their agents upon the tenants of these gentry, who were way-wardens of the district. But not one individual member of the Board offered a single reason why he should be thus expelled from office, although he publicly challenged them so to do. This outrageous violation of civil liberty took place in the neighbourhood of Monmouth. I will here quote an extract from a letter sent by the surveyor to the *Hereford Times*, touching this matter. It is dated February 12th, 1877, and is as follows :—

"*To the Editor of the* 'HEREFORD TIMES.'

"Sir,—Kindly allow me through the *Hereford Times* to say a few words to the ratepayers of the above district, and the public generally, respecting the treatment I, as Surveyor of the Highways, have received at the hands of the Board.

"For myself I can say without fear of contradiction, that, since I have held the office of surveyor, my object has been to do justice to the ratepayers and to those I employ on their behalf. But it has been my misfortune, from the time I became a candidate for the office, to meet with vexatious opposition from a certain quarter; I could never understand the reason why—except that I was unable to see through the blue spectacles of my opponents. The first step they took was to bring forward some one to oppose me. Failing to foist this candidate upon the public, they followed me with relentless opposition. which resulted in my expulsion from office by the exercise of a strong despotic influence over a considerable number of the way-wardens. And further, I have to complain that the Board has too readily yielded to the imperious dictation of my opponents—to the serious loss of the ratepayers, and the obstruction of the surveyor in the performance of his duties. And again, it would seem utterly incredible that when I received notice in October last to resign my office, on enquiring what charge they had against me, the then Chairman replied, 'We have no charge.' And no charge has been made against me at all. I therefore, consider that I have been treated most unfairly, and that the Board has acted in a most unEnglish and arbitrary manner."

The above episode conclusively shows the despotic influence brought to bear upon the political liberties of the people by those whose arbitrary power is obtained through the medium of the possession of a large monopoly of the land of the country. These are the men that assert on the political platform that landlords, farmers, and labourers sail in the same boat. But with the former it is a veritable pleasure-boat, scudding along gaily by the toil and skill of the latter, who are simply the humble oarsmen.

The gentlemen above referred to are fond of describing themselves as the friends of the farmers, and, since the labourers have obtained the franchise, they assert with coolness on the political platforms that the interests of the three parties are identical. But in what this likeness or identity consists is a puzzle difficult to unravel. The time of the gentry is spent mainly in scenes of sport and pleasure — horse-racing, steeple-chasing, hunting, shooting, games, and pleasures of all descriptions—with all the honours and privileges that wealth and position can command; whereas the farmer has the labour, care,

and anxiety, inevitably connected with the profitable and
also the unprofitable, management of the land, so as to be
able to find his landlord the necessary means of perpetua-
ting this mode of life, upon which landlords, as a rule, are
prone to embark. What identity of life is perceptible
between landlords and tenant-farmers? You may without
effort discern great diversity, or dissimilarity of life,
but the eye of an eagle would be unable to discover
identity. Now, if the farmer's identification with the landlord is so imperceptible, what shall we say as to the farm
labourer? Where is the congruity? where the coherence?
where the similarity? where the identity? Is it not a
monstrous sham, an intentional delusion and mockery, concocted to cheat and mislead the ignorant and weak-minded
working-man? With regard to the gentry referred to, I
have been struck with their religious habitudes and pretensions, seeing they pursue a daily course of worldly
pleasure incompatible with the recognised teachings of the
Christian religion. Yet these gentlemen stand forward as
the very champions of Church of England Christianity—
the pillars and mainstay thereof. For them and their
class she principally exists. Many of these gentlemen
will give a thousand or thousands of pounds at a time,
with a view to sustain this system for the purpose of
securing permanently the vast fund of wealth provided by
the State for the maintenance of the Church of England,
and which these gentlemen wish to preserve (they are
fond of preserves) as an hereditary source of wealth to
their kith and kin and fraternising adherents, in per-
petuity. Is this the upshot of Christianity, I would ask,
in this the last decade of the nineteenth century? Tell it
not in Gath, many a Christian would say; but it is too
late, for it is well known from Dan to Beersheba—from
John O'Groats to Land's End. And how can honest men
receive it? with cordial reception or virtuous indignation?
Some remarks on my experience relative to the contests that
took place in our neighbourhood touching the question of
Church-rates, prior to their abolition, may be relevant here.
In an adjoining parish in which I was eligible as a vestry-
man, and in which I took a lively interest, the clergy
and their churchwardens were determined to impose this
payment upon Nonconformists and Churchmen alike. The
Nonconformists very naturally resisted the unjust and

unrighteous imposition. The anti-Church-rate party in this parish were fortunate in being led by a veteran endowed with the right qualities. He was a freeholder and farmer, and independent in both circumstances and mind. He was not to be drawn aside from his purpose by soft or smooth words, nor frightened by the frowns and raillery of his opponents. He would stir up his army time after time, and bring them to battle, inspiring them with the same spirit of enthusiasm as his own. We entitled him "Our Garibaldi" as a mark of respect for his courage and thoroughness. Unfortunately, the country is exceedingly barren of such men, or we should soon obtain more even-handed justice. The Church-rate party had also the advantage of having a leader of great mental ability, but these are not always the most useful or valuable men, but oftentimes the most dangerous to the interests of the people. This gentleman, who was the vicar of an adjoining parish, and considered an able clergyman, was described by an old churchwarden of his parish "as a good man in the Church but a devil out." Whenever he attended our vestry he always occupied the chair. He would put a motion to the meeting or refuse it if it was not agreeable to his sweet will. He was thoroughly aristocratic, lived in a seat of his own, and was quite a chum with the leading gentry all round. He had a wife, but no issue ; but, notwithstanding his enviable position, he was not content therewith. A living of greater value and importance than his own having become vacant, he could not resist applying for it, conscious that his influence with the patron was sufficient to procure it for himself. He therefore threw up the charge of curing the souls he had undertaken to cure, that he might obtain more wealth, or what was formerly described by Christian teachers as " filthy lucre," but is now become the principal desideratum of the Christian ministry belonging to the Church of England. The patron above referred to has several livings in his gift, but to describe him as a religious man would be a misnomer ; his life being spent in absolute worldly pleasure, consisting of all the frivolities, pastimes, sports, and gambling connected with the turf, known as fast life. And to men of this description of character is handed over, by the constitution of the Church of England, the presentation of livings, or, as it is called, the cure of souls, which he gives to a relative, a friend, a crony, or the friend of a crony, who, if he is a sporting character, will be the more eligible for the presentation. How are we, as reasonable people, to look upon such grotesque, incongruous, incoherent, and inconsistent dealing with religion? Are we to look up to such a religious establishment with equanimity? or rather would it not be more in accord with moral principles to meet it with indignant reprobation, as adapted to create hypocrisy, and bring about the demoralisation of society? Was it to establish a religious system of this character, so diametrically antagonistic to the ethical teachings of the New Testament, so much at variance with the precepts and example of Christ himself, that he sacrificed the glories of heaven, descended into this world and became a poor persecuted man, not having where to lay his head, and spent his life in the service of the poor, whilst he preached against the acquisition of riches? Was it for the purpose of establishing and consolidating a system of religion such as the Church of England presents to the world, with all its wealth, pomposity, arrogance, dominance, intolerance, and inequality, that Christ made all the sacrifices attributed to him? Was it to accomplish this object that he suffered a life of martyrdom and died a painful and ignominious death upon the cross? What answer can be given to these plain crucial questions? Having given these matters serious consideration and reflected upon religion as represented by the Church of England, and compared it, to the best of my judgment, with the moral teachings advanced by Christ himself and approved and appreciated by moral men generally, I became amazed at its dissimilarity, its virtual antagonism, its pretentiousness, hollowness, and conventionalism. It is an obvious fact that a formal recognition of these pretensions and submission to these hypocrisies and formalisms are the stepping-stones to respectability and worldly promotion. This is the moral state and condition of society to-day, after being under the patronage and protection of the Church of England for hundreds of years, whilst it devours millions of money, annually provided by the toil and industry of the labouring class to keep such a system afloat.

I have a strong and weighty charge against the Church

of England, viz., that of being constitutionally adapted to become the greatest habitation or reservoir of infidelity that the country can produce. Its efficiency and success in this respect need not be questioned. I will here quote a letter to the *Hereford Times*, dated August 12th, 1891, which will help to elucidate and confirm what I advance. It is as follows:

" SIR,—The newspaper press reports the following noteworthy declaration as that of the Bishop of St. Asaph, viz., ' That, during the short time he has been at St. Asaph, sixteen Nonconformist ministers, some of them men of the first rank, have applied to him for Holy Orders.' The validity of this statement may pass unquestioned, extraordinary as it may appear from different points of view ; but it would be interesting to know the paramount cause that induced these Nonconformist preachers to seek to become ministers in the Church of England. We do not find them pressing into the Church of Rome, neither do we find Church clergymen pressing into the Dissenting Churches. What, then, is the powerful stimulus that inspires this eager hankering after the Church ? Surely it does not consist in a conviction that the Church of England follows upon the lines of primitive Christianity in closer proximity than those of the Dissenting churches. If such were really the inducement, we might admire their Christian sincerity, consistency, and integrity, even if we failed to be convinced of the wisdom of their judgment. But I am strongly of the opinion that the prevailing impulse Churchwards by these gentlemen does not arise from the promptings of Christian faith, but contrariwise, from a virtual abandonment thereof, with a disposition to adopt a time-serving conventional policy with ease and independence as the end in view, and all the respectability (sham or otherwise) that such a course is calculated to produce. We talk glibly about the scepticism and infidelity of the age, but where can we find infidelity in all its naked deformity such as this ? Does it not then behove us as a progressive and intelligent people to consider the justice, utility, consistency, and morality of upholding a national system of religion which from its nature and constitution is eminently adapted to draw within its sphere men of all descriptions of character, men destitute of even a modicum of veneration for the principles of truth, justice, and consistency ? It has been my lot to compulsorily support clergymen for scores of years, not one of whom as a religious, moral, and intellectual man was worthy to fill the post he occupied as instructor of the people. And I may further add that I have known several Dissenters, and as such very zealous in religious matters ; but something crossed their path, and they withdrew from Dissent, and then appeared occasionally in church, taking no active part in religion beyond a formal acquiescence. Religion and they had really parted company. Thus we find the Church of England an accommodating receptacle for all parties, from the most faithful devotee to the most abandoned impostor, and this demoralising system is upheld by the wealth of the nation, wrung from the sons and daughters of toil. Is not this a matter which demands the serious attention of the best of men?—A FARMER."

I remember on a certain occasion that my home was visited by three Dissenting ministers (Congregationalists) my mother being of that persuasion. The conversation turned one day upon witchcraft, which my mother maintained was proved by the case of the Witch of Endor. To this the ministers appeared to have nothing to say, but laughed secretly at my mother's credulity. But these gentlemen had a secret in hand which they were reluctant to reveal. One of the three was on the point of leaving his own Church for that of the Church of England; this was the great secret of their conversation. I feel quite sure that another of the trio, if not all of them, would have gone too, were it not for the great unpleasantness and difficulty connected with the severance from old friends. And now I ask my Christian friends whether the attitude of these preachers bespoke a lively faith in the Christian religion, or rather a virtual abandonment thereof? And I here remark that men, and women too, possessed of common sense and reasoning powers, should use those powers themselves in deciding what is right or wrong relative to religion, and not depute this important duty to any priesthood whatever, be their pretensions ever so imposing, inasmuch as these priesthoods manage to obtain an easy, sometimes a gay, luxurious life themselves by instilling their different theories into the minds of the people, whether true or false, whilst the people have to do all the drudgery and slavery, and are advised by these teachers therewith to be content. I have observed one thing as a matter of notoriety both in Church-people and Nonconformists, which is, that the laity manifest greater sincerity and religious devotion than do their pastors. I have witnessed this among Dissenters, but much more in connection with the Church. I have known many clergymen whose general conduct testifies to the fact that they care nothing about the religious affairs of the people or the Church. Feeling persuaded that the living they hold they shall enjoy during their time, they have no further care. I have been acquainted with some religious professors, both Churchmen and Dissenters, whose lives corresponded with their profession, and approximated as far as practicable to consistency of character. There are a variety of motives that induce people to countenance religion, besides a pious belief in its genuineness. Among others may be mentioned the desire to be respectable. I was once acquainted with a farmer, considered quite respectable. He was a Church-born man. He would go to Church every Sunday morning, taking his sons with him ; but if they were not ready when he was they had to submit to oaths and cuffs, which he dealt out to them to his heart's content. The remainder of the day would be spent in the company of friends and the enjoyment of pipe and glass. Not a bad type, this, of a Church-going farmer, with plenty of means. But there are other inducements of a more tangible character for upholding the Church, in-ducements sufficient to arrest and absorb the attention of the nobility of the country, viz., the vast revenue provided by the State for the support of the Church ; and which earls, lords, and the aristocracy generally covet, and there-fore press themselves into the Church, to share its patronage and monopolise its most lucrative livings. What harmony or congruity, what fidelity to Christian teachings can be discerned in such a procedure when the record says that Jesus informed his disciples that it was a most difficult thing for a rich man to inherit the kingdom of Heaven ? Also that, if you desire to become a disciple, you are directed to sell all you have and give it the poor, and take up your cross and follow him. Again, there is another section of Church adherents that play an active part in Church maintenance, induced, as it would appear, by secular combined with religious motives. I chiefly allude to lay members of the Church, some of whom I have known from my youth as extremely zealous in the interests of the Church, even where the clergy were apathetic or utterly indifferent. I have known them visit the neighbours frequently, distribute tracts, invite the people to Church, urge them to christen their infants and to get them confirmed, and thence to the communion-table. The motives were of a twofold character; they had a reference to the good things of this life (or the bird in hand) and also to a future state (or the one in the bush). I always observed that zeal, pushed resolutely in a persistent manner, was productive of considerable evil as the source of much deceit and hypocrisy. This is quite evident in any neighbourhood where wealthy families reside that are strong active Church adherents, zealously countenancing everything favourable to Church interests, but discountenancing anything that does not chime in therewith. Here we find hypocrisy growing freely, as though it had found a suitable soil for its development. But if a wealthy family should be also generous-hearted and liberal to those that conform to their wishes, you will find the locality in which they move to be a very hotbed of hypocrisy. Such a state of things is productive of great evil, which no amount of devotion to any religious ideas can counterbalance, as it has an inevitable tendency to weaken and undermine the moral powers, which are sufficiently weak at best, without any bribery or temptation thereto. When I was a child attending Sunday-school, we had a wealthy family residing in our parish who were liberal to the poor and respected all round. They were rigidly Church, one of them being a Church minister, but the neighbours all round seemed to live in general awe of them, as may be gathered from the following fact. During the stay of this family in their country seat the church would be well filled, both by farmers and labourers, nearly all of whom were their tenants. But when the family left for London, as they frequently did during the winter season, the church would scarce have an occupant except parson, clerk, and children. This goes to illustrate the evils of Church or sectarian supremacy, and its tendency to the demoralisation of the people.

The elevating religious dogmas above moral principles accounts for the great amount of deception that generally prevails, and the shameless hypocrisy with which society abounds. It is commenced in our schools, when the minds of the children are tender and receptive of good or evil. I have had the privilege and honor of filling the office of a member of a School Board for a period of fifteen years, during which time there was nothing that disturbed or marred the unanimity and harmony of the Board but the persistent attempts to introduce into the school religious or sectarian influence. This was the only apple of discord with which we had to deal. In earlier life, when I was a Church attendant and a chorister, I cannot say that I was ever fully satisfied with the Church as a religious institution, notwithstanding my high regard for many Church people as individuals. My observation and reflection led me to the conclusion that the Church by no means held up a lofty ideal to the aspirations of the people, but contrariwise, that it has a strong tendency to create formalism and destroy moral instincts from infancy upwards. In proof of this it is only necessary to take notice of the procedure of the Church with regard to the initiation of its members. The unconscious babe, agreeably to Church formalism, is presented at church to the minister, who takes possession of it, puts water on its face, a cross on its forehead, recites a few prayers, and formally dedicates the irresponsible child into the membership of the Church by the repetition of the formula, "I baptize thee in the name of the Father, and of the Son, and of the Holy Ghost. Amen." Now we find that the Church maintains that through the performance of this ceremony the child has really become regenerate, or born again. There is abundant proof in the baptismal services to verify what I say. I will give but one quotation. It is from the Private Baptism of Infants. The minister, having satisfied himself that the child has already been christened, delivers himself as follows:

"I certify you, that in this case all is well done, and according unto due order, concerning the baptizing of this child; who, being born in original sin and in the wrath of God, is now by the laver of regeneration in baptism received into the number of the children of God, and heirs of everlasting life."

Now, to my mind, it is a matter of vast importance to ascertain the accuracy of these pretensions—pretensions of such vast importance that they should not be treated in any way approaching indifference,—pretensions that, if true, demand our most serious and devout attention. But if false, what shall we say of it? How shall we find language adequate to condemn such imposition?

There is an accurate way of testing this matter, like other matters, by the observation of results. There are no other feasible means of arriving at a sound conclusion. If it can be made apparent that children passing through the process of Church baptism have obtained some regenerative advantages that distinguish them from others who have not submitted to this baptismal process, then I admit that the advocates and promoters of the system are justified in the course they pursue. But if, on the other hand, these Church-baptised children fail to distinguish themselves in morals from others who, in position and advantages are alike, but have never been baptised, what honest conclusion is it possible to arrive at? If, as is maintained, the regeneration produced by this baptism makes of its recipients new creatures, it would be interesting to know in what this newness consists, for it is quite obvious that children having the same advantages, whether baptised or unbaptised, are as regards their moral condition quite upon a par.

I do not for a moment insinuate that children of Church people are in any respect inferior to other children; but neither have they by baptism obtained any superiority of a moral or (if you like) a spiritual character above or beyond the unbaptised. In what, then, does this assumed change manifest itself? In my humble judgment it does not manifest itself at all—except as a monstrous imposition, discreditable to any Church or community of people. It is rotten at the core. And yet this holy ordinance of baptism is the very foundation of the Church of England. Upon this basis its superstructure is built; and, if the basis be as here described, what confidence can be reposed in all other forms, ceremonies, sacraments, and pretensions that rest upon such a foundation? And that I have not misrepresented the case will be apparent to all that will give the matter a candid, unprejudiced, and impartial examination; and I think they will inevitably arrive at the conclusion that the system is hollow and deceptive. Of what value then, I would ask, is the Church of England, the source and depôt of much of the injustice by which the country is afflicted? Were it not for greed of the gold which the Church so abundantly supplies out of her ill-gotten stores she would lose followers in the face of all the competition and counter-attraction of worldly things. For after all it is gold, silver, and copper that are the trinity in unity that commands the most ardent worship. Notwithstanding my early connection with the Church and friendliness with some of its best upholders, I could but regard her as much like the Church of Laodicea, neither cold nor hot — religious formalism and ceremonies standing out as her most conspicuous features; and I should have long ago separated myself from her connection. were it not that I was held back by the good fellowship and influence of kind friends who were financially interested in her maintenance. This separation took place about 1838, when I was twenty-four years old. I then gave religious matters more serious thought. Hitherto I had simply acquiesced in the elementary teachings of the Christian religion as held by Protestants generally ; but now I became more impressed with the importance of religion as represented by earnest religious advocates. I reasoned that, if religion was worth anything at all, it demanded our most sincere and persistent devotion, and as Nonconformity presented itself to my mind as approximating more closely to the moral teachings of Christ and the method of the primitive Churches in the voluntary support of religion, contrasting, as it does, with the compulsory method pursued by the Church of England for its sustentation, I felt that I could n•t conscientiously stand by it any longer, my past experience with regard to the Church contributing largely to this decision; and having been attracted by the apparent earnestness, sincerity, and devotion to religion of some of my acquaintance connected with the Congregational Church, I was induced to cast in my lot with them, which I did with considerable earnestness and sincerity.

Our first minister was not a very popular one with us ; therefore he soon left the church ; but his successor was well received, and became a favorite with many. He was by no means a *Boanerges*, or son of thunder, but one disposed to dwell upon the bright side of religion, entitling him to rank as a son of *consolation*. This minister was fond of taking his hearers up into the ethereal regions. He delighted to expatiate upon the blessings that were in store for us, the favoured children of God. He would dilate with enthusiasm on the blessings and eternal joy which God had provided for us, and how we should bask beneath the eternal sunshine of his presence. We should have as our companions angels, archangels, and the spirits of just men made perfect. We should be honoured with the company of Abraham, Isaac, and Jacob, the holy prophets and martyrs of every age ; and we should behold the Lord Jesus as he is, and he would lead us from fountain to fountain of living water, and he would carry us through immensity from planet to planet, from sphere to sphere, and unravel to us the mysteries of creation and his redeeming love. We should also have the distinguished honour and pleasure of casting our crowns at his feet and pacing the golden streets of the new Jerusalem, with the comforting assurance that God would wipe away tears from our eyes. Such bright enchanting prospects would occasionally produce a flood of tears, accompanied by smiles of joy from his most sensitive hearers. This playing upon the sentiments of the people by the Christian ministry is by no means uncommon in all denominations. Neither is it harmful, when it does not extinguish or smother our rational and moral instincts. But observation proves that there is great danger here. For myself I can say that, captivating and ensnaring as sentimental teachings are, they have not been able wholly to command the reasoning powers which should predominate and rule all. Reason was the key that undid the lock of Doubting Castle for my reception. I compared the general conduct of religious professors with those that made no profession at all, and the distinction between them I found to be imperceptible. Oftentimes the preference, if any, had to be given to the non-professor, and yet the professor claimed eternal happiness beyond the grave and consigned his neighbour, who might be a much better man than himself, to the bitter pains of eternal death. What cause can be assigned for this outrageous distinction? The only proffered reply we obtain is in the record, "He that believeth and is baptised shall be saved: but he that believeth not shall be damned." If these terrible words are true, of course they are as operative to-day as they were nearly 1,900 years ago. Does it not require a large amount of credulity to make a rational and humane being digest a dogma or theory of this description? There are other passages of scripture coincident with the above, such as, "many are called but few are chosen," and "broad is the way that leads to destruction, and many there be that go in thereat. But strait is the gate and narrow the way that leads to life, and few there are that find it." There is the evil; it is of this very narrowness of the way that I complain. It is too narrow, too exclusive, too inadequate, to meet the exigencies of mankind. The saving of a small minority, and the damning of a vast majority, is in direct incongruity with our reasoning powers, and humane proclivities. I had rather lie down for ever in the sleep of death without any hope of immortality than risk the chance of being saved among the few, or damned with the vast majority, as portrayed by our religious teachers. After having battled secretly for some time with my conflicting ideas, I ventured to lay my case before our minister, which he listened to with much concern, but utterly failed to supply any antidote to the misgivings and doubts already engendered. The policy he pursued on that occasion was to point out other difficulties and mysteries equal to my own, and which he used as an argument to me to smother or suppress my own doubts and difficulties. But as I knew nothing of two blacks producing a white I did not adopt his policy. Then he endeavoured to persuade me that the ideas and impressions upon my mind were the work of the devil. Well, I hold that if the devil influences the minds of men to use their reasoning powers with regard to religion and also to cultivate a philanthropic spirit towards mankind, he is not such a bad devil after all. We have many in human form that fall far beneath him.

The terrible consequences associated with religion as presented in the Christian scriptures are so grave and great that it behoves every person to satisfy himself, or herself, as to the veracity of their contents. Impressed with this idea I thought well to review the life of Jesus Christ as contained in the Gospels, and, taking the Gospel of St. Luke, I found in the first chapter two remarkable narratives delivered, in which the Angel Gabriel figures. The first narrative has reference to the birth of John the Baptist, and is of such a novel and extraordinary character that it highly taxes human credibility. The next narrative relates to the birth and destiny of Jesus Christ, and is of a still more extraordinary character. We find it represented that an angel of God called Gabriel came to Nazareth and appeared to a virgin named Mary, and, after saluting her, delivered his message, which was to the following effect: "That she should conceive and bring forth a son, and should call his name Jesus. And that he should be great, and should be called the son of the highest: and the Lord God would give unto him the throne of his father David." I regard this passage of scripture as of immense importance, conjointly with others of similar import, as furnishing us with satisfactory proof of Jesus Christ's mission in life. Mary appeared surprised and astonished, as well she might, and innocently inquired thus: "How can these things be, seeing I know not a man?" To which the Angel, in the 35th verse of this chapter, replied. It may be in an angelic or heavenly fashion, but certainly neither in dialect nor ideas is it consonant with modern usage nor human experience. That Mary was a decorous person I take for granted, and I have a strong impression that she was extremely modest; a quality, by the way, calculated to prove much more disastrous to anyone than beneficial, although a moderate share of this virtue is admirable and commendable in all.

Many years ago I knew a couple of young people who kept each other's company some time, they were decent and respectable in their sphere of life. But the young woman became unwell. Her mother took her to the doctor, who prescribed for the young woman, assuring her mother that she would be better by-and-bye. The young couple soon got married, and in a short time the doctor was sent for. The young woman was confined, and the doctor made a remark respecting her child. She denied that the child was hers; positively denied it. "Well, my good woman," jocularly replied the doctor, "it must be either yours or mine." When young women thus constituted fall into trouble previous to marriage, no one can account for what they will say or do to screen themselves. Their imagination and invention will be taxed to the utmost, and their veracity will often fail in the presence of their distress. In this long chapter, the first of St. Luke, amongst other extraordinary matters our attention is drawn to an old Jewish priest named Zacharias—whose wife's name was Elizabeth. This lady was a cousin to Mary the mother of Jesus Christ, and it would appear that they were on very intimate terms—as may be gathered from the following circumstance,—that as soon as Mary had been apprised by the Angel that she should ere long become the mother

of a child she betook herself into the hill country with
haste into a city of Judea, and entered into the house of
Zacharias, and saluted Elizabeth, and took up her abode
there for three months before she returned to her own
house. In this remarkable chapter we are also supplied
with singular speeches,—one by Elizabeth, one by Mary,
and one by Zacharias—but they all partake of a sacer-
dotal flavour. It is a matter of curiosity to us in the
present day as to how these speeches became known to
posterity. Who recorded them when delivered? There
would be no shorthand reporter present. And these
speeches, if delivered as recorded, were uttered before the
birth of Christ, but were not given to the world by the
writers of the Gospels for years after the death of Christ,
so that there was plenty of time and opportunity to render
them suitable to any change of circumstance. Now
Zacharias was not only a priest, but a prophet, holding
with Jesus that a prophet is not without honour, except
in his own country and by those acquainted with him.
The reasons are obvious. If the prophecies are true, the
prophet would not fail to find honour, but being false they
are treated with contempt. I have known some who,
having professed to be charmers and conjurers, were
thought much of by many in the distance, but all in the
neighbourhood, except the very superstitious, ridiculed
their pretensions.

In this prophecy, so-called, of Zacharias he refers to
the Lord God of Israel as having "raised up an horn of
salvation for us in the house of his servant David . . . .
and also that we should be saved from our enemies and
from the hand of all that hate us. . . . . And that he
would grant unto us that we, being delivered out of the
hand of our enemies, might serve him without fear."
The annunciation of the angel to Mary is prophetic
respecting her son, when he affirms that God would give
unto him the throne of his father David. Further, the
reference made by Zacharias, just quoted, points in the
same direction, and I think that, in glancing at the life of
Christ from now onwards, we should bear in mind what is
here indicated, as we shall find as we advance much that
will coincide with and corroborate it. We find that at
eight days old Jesus was circumcised, in accordance with
the Jewish rites. Shortly after we find his parents taking

him to Jerusalem to present him to the Lord, and to offer
as a sacrifice a pair of turtle doves, or two young pigeons,
according to the law of Moses.   We learn nothing further
of the child Jesus until he is twelve years old, when his
parents take him with them to the Feast of the Passover
at Jerusalem.   But when they returned homewards they,
with very culpable negligence, left the young boy behind,
and travelled a day's journey without missing him, although such an extraordinary child.   Then they had to
return in search of him, and it took three days to find
him.   This did not show much parental care on the part
of the parents nor filial duty on the part of their son.
Nevertheless, they found him in the temple, sitting in the
midst of the doctors, both hearing and asking them questions.   It would be a matter of curiosity to-day, if not
advantage, could we ascertain the import of those questions and answers then and there produced.   We now
wholly lose sight of Jesus for the long period of eighteen
years.   How was he engaged all this time?. Was it in
following his trade as a carpenter?   Whether we regard
his mission in life as that of the savior of mankind from
everlasting death, or as the future king of Israel, whose
object it was to occupy the throne of David and redeem
the Israelites out of the hand of their enemies—either
way this reticence for so long a period by a person of such
significant pretensions is hardly adapted to inspire the
world with confidence.   In referring to the great Tichborne case we are aware that the claimant maintained
silence for about twenty years before putting in his claim
to the Tichborne estate as the veritable "Sir Roger"—
with what results the country has long been cognizant.
To protect ourselves against impositions shows prudence.
I have often wondered at the great blank of eighteen
years in the history of the life of an individual of such
extraordinary pretensions.   This thorough silence for so
long a period threw doubt upon the history, and demanded
some explanation; which, by the way, I never found
Christian ministers attempt to give.   But recently, in an
article in the *Hereford Times* newspaper of March 24th,
1894, I find a curious explanation given which, if true,
fills up the gap in the life of Christ, and at any rate
suggests much that is coincident and coherent with our
Gospels.   In the article referred to, which is headed "The

Life of Christ in Thibet," we find that a Russian traveller of the name of M. Nicholas Notovitch heard in a monastery that the Buddhists knew and honored the prophet Issa. Certain particulars of the life of Issa forced upon him the conviction that this prophet was Jesus Christ, who, according to this history, was born in Israel, but fled from his parents at thirteen years of age, and went with merchants to Sindh. At fourteen he was living among the Aryas. He learnt to read and understand the Vedas. He was initiated in the mysteries of pure Buddhism. Then he went westwards, preaching against idols. In Persia he opposed the religion of Zoroaster, but he was persecuted by magicians, and fled. He was twenty-nine years of age when he returned to Judea. This just fills the blank in the history of the life of Christ. It is said that Issa at once on entering Judea began to preach, but his popularity alarmed Pontius Pilate, and the governor, fearing a mutiny, caused Issa to be imprisoned, tortured, and tried before the Sanhedrim. A witness also was called who, speaking to Issa, said : "Did you not claim to be the king of Israel when you said that the Lord of Heaven had sent you to prepare his people?" We further find that Issa was crucified with two thieves, and that his sepulchre was found open and empty afterwards.

The life of Christ as given in the Gospels very conclusively shows that Christ was impressed with the idea that he was to become the future king of Israel. How could he escape from such a conclusion if he believed his mother's tale about the visit of the angel Gabriel, the supernatural conception, and the prophecies of Zacharias respecting him? It is but reasonable that his mind would be impressed by their tutelage into a lively desire to realise those predictions. Hence we find so much in his history that cannot be accounted for on any other ground. I take in the first place the case of Zebedee's children. The mother brought her two sons with her to Jesus, desiring him that they should sit the one on his right hand and the other on his left in his kingdom. To this important inquiry Jesus expressed no surprise ; received it as an appropriate question ; but intimated that, though not within his province to grant the favour, he desired it should be given to those whom the father chose. And in the nineteenth chapter of Matthew Christ tells his dis-

ciples that those that follow him in the regeneration
(whatever he meant by it), when the son of man shall sit
on the throne of his glory, they also shall sit on twelve
thrones judging the twelve tribes of Israel. And everyone
that forsakes houses, or brethren, or sisters, or father, or
mother, or wife, or children, or lands for his name's sake,
shall receive an hundred-fold, and shall inherit eternal
life. This appeared a strong temptation to espouse the
cause of Christ, and cast in their lot with him; but it
seems the people were restrained by unbelief. Even his
natural brothers did not believe in him (see St. John).
But others had some confused belief in him; Nathaniel,
for instance, who addressed Christ as "Rabbi, thou art
the Son of God; thou art the king of Israel." And in
the twelfth chapter of St. John we have the account of
much people bearing branches of palm trees and going
forth to meet Jesus, crying: "Hosanna! Blessed is the
King of Israel, that cometh in the name of the Lord."
Jesus also rode upon an ass into Jerusalem that a prophecy might be fulfilled, which says: "Tell ye the
daughter of Sion, behold, thy king cometh unto thee,
meek, and sitting upon an ass, and the colt the foal of an
ass." Now it appears that there was a very pronounced
conviction running through Judea that Jesus was a candidate for the kingdom of Israel. This conviction was shared
by his friends and enemies, and fostered by his own words
and deeds. Even the chief priests and Pharisees held
a council against him, "fearing that if he were left alone
the Romans would come and take away both their place
and nation." So strongly were some of the people persuaded that Jesus was to be their king and deliverer that
they were disposed, on one occasion, to come and take him
by force. And on the occasion of the trial of Jesus the
Jews warned Pilate that, if he released Jesus, he was
no friend of Cæsar's, for whosoever maketh himself
a king speaketh against Cæsar. Even the soldiers
that plaited a crown of thorns for his head hailed
him in derision as "King of the Jews," and, when
crucified, a superscription was written over him in letters
of Greek, Latin, and Hebrew, "This is the King of
the Jews." Jesus then, instead of ascending the throne
of David according to the expectation and hopes of his
friends, died upon the Cross as an impostor or pre-

tender. Even his disciples forsook him and fled when
the hour of trial came, notwithstanding all their pro-
fessions of loyalty or avowed belief in him and his
miracles. Well, Christ's mission as the presumptive King
of Israel having wholly failed, his followers invented a
scheme to cover their retreat. They now say that he
(Christ) came to die for the sins of the world. Had
Christ succeeded in his attempt to obtain the throne of
Israel, we never should have heard that the salvation of
the world was to be obtained by the shedding of the
blood of Christ, and by no other means. For my own
part, it is utterly incomprehensible why mankind could
not obtain free pardon for all their misdeeds, especially if
we grant that mankind is the product of the handiwork
of God, fashioned after his own likeness. There is
nothing derogatory to an individual in performing acts
of pardon, but it exhibits magnanimity, generosity, and
amiability of character. But to represent God as a
revengeful being who could not forgive the faults of his
imperfect creatures without having an innocent person
sacrificed (and that person his own son) for his gratification, appears to me as a moral anomaly unworthy the
recognition of moral beings. I have never been able to
recognise the value of blood as a sacrifice, its meritorious
quality and efficacy, but it seems to have been an
indispensable requisite among the priesthoods of all ages
and nations. But are the Scriptures uniform in their maintenance of the doctrine that mankind (if lost) must be
saved by a bloody sacrifice only, or not saved at all? In
the 15th chapter of St. Luke Jesus Christ, who says he
came from God, and therefore knows his will and disposition, gives a representation of God's treatment of his
erring creatures, which may be summed up as a free,
full, and loving pardon without any sacrifice. What
more is required in regard to this matter? It is a correct
representation, or it is not. Jesus Christ is responsible
for it. Would he give us a false representation?

In this chapter Jesus Christ has given a most amiable
description of the Deity. He is here represented as a
loving Father, delighted to pardon and welcome his erring,
repentant children, without any sacrifice or compensation
whatever on their part, or that of anyone else. Now the
crucial question is: Did Jesus Christ give in this chapter

a correct portraiture of God the Father as to his dealings towards mankind ? If this is so, it appears to me to be a doctrine that would meet with very general recognition and appreciation. Or are we to conclude that Jesus has not given us here a true representation of God's dealings with his creatures ? If he gave a correct account, what bocomes of the atonement by the blood of Jesus Christ? Is not the free mercy of God quite adequate to human necessities ? But there are other teachings in the Scriptures quite in harmony with that just given—such as "Blessed are the merciful, for they shall obtain mercy." And again, "If ye forgive men their trespasses, your heavenly Father will also forgive yours." Without any sacrifice whatever; no blood, no agony, no sorrow or pain ; none asked for, none required. But to return prior to the Crucifixion. It is quite obvious to all that Christ failed in his attempt to obtain the coveted throne of David, notwithstanding his ambition and the encouragement he must have received from his friends and abettors from early childhood. He had unusual faith in God, perhaps fostered by the extraordinary communications of his mother and friends, touching his birth and prospects. But it is quite apparent that, as his end drew nigh, things began to wear a very gloomy aspect indeed. He had been impressed with the idea that he could command legions of angels from heaven to his rescue, but when the time of his great trouble drew nigh he found himself deserted both by men and angels ; even the staunchest of his own disciples denied, betrayed, and forsook him. And when he saw that no relief came from any quarter, but that he was wholly given up to his enemies and had to suffer the dreadful death of a crucifixion upon the Cross—in despair he cried with a loud voice, "My God, My God, why hast thou forsaken me ?" What is the natural and relevant construction to be placed upon such an exclamation under the circumstances ? Is it not that of a man labouring under a consciousness of great disappointment? as must have inevitably been the case if Christ believed the statement of the angel Gabriel delivered to his mother previous to his birth, in which it was announced that the Lord God would give unto him the throne of his father David, and in which he (Christ) appears to have placed great confidence. But, instead of being elevated, according to ex-

pectation, to the throne of his father David, he had to
submit to the torture and degradation of death upon the
Cross—which was highly calculated to produce that significant and unhappy exclamation, " My God, My God, why
hast thou forsaken me ?" It is noteworthy that the
mother of Jesus, although called a virgin, and an im-
maculate virgin to this day, was nevertheless a mother of
a large family, consisting of at least five sons and two
daughters. Jesus being the eldest son, followed by James
and Joses, Simon and Judas, they had also sisters, but
their names or number are not given. But a circumstance
of a more noteworthy character still may be referred to,
which is that Christ's own natural brothers did not believe
in him; see St. John, chapter 7, verse 5. How was it
that his brothers did not believe in him ? Did they not
believe their mother with regard to the important
announcement of the Angel ?

We find that, after the death of Jesus Christ, his followers
circulated the report that he was risen again from the
dead, and that he had appeared to many of them, and
that he had ascended into heaven with infinite power,
and that his mission to this world, after all, was not to
become king of Israel and to rescue them out of the
hands of their enemies; but to redeem mankind by his
blood from sin and its consequences. And the idea is
current that Christ is this day acting as our mediator,
and pleading our cause in the presence of God. We have
seen that the mission of Christ as candidate for the throne
of Israel has utterly failed. We will now test the con-
tention of his followers, that Christ's real mission to this
world was to save mankind from eternal damnation. It
will be admitted all round that Christ must have been
very anxious to redeem mankind from their imputed position of being under the wrath of God, or he would never
have made the wonderful sacrifice he did on their account.
For is it not reasonable that he would put that power in
operation and secure the salvation of mankind ? Now the
grand question is, Is there any proof that Christ exercises
the attributes of power with which it is affirmed he is
invested, in carrying out that plan of salvation said to be
necessary for the redemption of mankind ? The world
to-day presents but one answer and that an emphatically
negative one. It is agreeable neither to reason nor
common-sense that an individual would sacrifice the most

consummate happiness for thirty-three years, and descend into a low state of existence, accompanied by poverty, disrespect, and insult, and ultimately submit to a most painful death to accomplish some lasting good to mankind, and then, having been invested with the power to carry it out, neglects or refuses to exercise that power. Such conduct is tantamount to that of Christ's as displayed with regard to the salvation of the human race. To prove this it is only necessary to cast an eye upon the present religious and moral condition of the world after nearly 1900 years of Christian teaching. According to Christian computation, the human race, in the year of Christ 1884, amounted to 1,440,000,000. Of these there were 440,000,000 of nominal Christians, whilst the non-Christians amounted to 1,000,000,000; so that a large proportion of the human population have never yet heard of the glad tidings, if such a term, under such conditions, can be considered any way appropriate. In "Veritas's" "Conventional Christianity," written to the Churches of the empire with the consent of the Archbishop of Canterbury, it is asserted, that it is to be feared that a very small fraction of professing Christians have experienced the saving power of religion. All the above goes to show the terrible dilemma in which mankind is placed, admitting that Christianity is founded on truth.

As rational beings, possessed of moral sentiments, how are we to receive the doctrines comprised in the term "Christianity"? Are we to believe that Jesus Christ had so much love for the human race that he made all the sacrifices attributed to him, yet now that he has risen from the dead and gone to heaven, possessed of almighty power, this love has collapsed, or become so inoperative that he can view with complacency, daily, millions of sensitive souls take up for ever their abode in the regions of eternal damnation? All the time, forsooth, he possesses the power to mould the heart, regenerate the spirit, and treat mankind as clay in the hands of the potter, without any sacrifice on his part whatever! Is this such treatment as we should expect from a Saviour attached to the human race and anxious for its salvation? But we are cautioned by our Christian advocates not to trust to our reason in religious matters, although it is the grandest endowment of which human nature can boast. But why should we fear to trust our reason in religious matters more than

secular ones? We upbraid and reproach ourselves and
others when our words or actions are at variance with the
dictates of reason, and I am convinced that it shows great
impotency in any religious system that shrinks from the
presence of the attribute of reason. But if Christianity
cannot stand the test of reason it is quite at home in
the region of sentiment, and assumes that there is a
heavenly treasure in the keeping of the Church: an
assumption which Mr. Gladstone, in his religious controversy with Colonel Ingersoll, endeavoured to maintain.
Touching this matter, I will here give a short extract from
the Colonel's reply to Mr. Gladstone. (The whole of the
reply is well worth reading; its price is fourpence, and it
is published in London, at 28, Stonecutter Street, E.C.)
The extract is as follows :—

" What is the treasure in the keeping of the Church? Let
me tell you. It is this. That there is but one true religion—
Christianity—and that all others are false; that the prophets,
and Christs, and priests of all others have been and are impos-
tors, or the victims of insanity; that the Bible is the one in-
spired book—the one authentic record of the words of God;
that all men are naturally depraved and deserve to be punished
with unspeakable torments for ever; that there is only one
path that leads to heaven, while countless highways lead to
hell; that there is only one name under heaven by which a
human being can be saved; that we must believe in the Lord
Jesus Christ; that this life, with its few and fleeting years,
fixes the fate of man; that the few will be saved, and the
many lost for ever. This is the heavenly treasure within the
keeping of your Church."

And this "treasure" has been guarded by the cherubim
of persecution, whose flaming swords were wet for many
centuries with the best and bravest blood. It has been
guarded by cunning, by hypocrisy, by mendacity, by
perfidy, by calumniating the generous, by maligning the
good, by thumbscrews and racks, by Holy Inquisitions, by
robbery and assassination, by poison and fire, by the virtues
of the ignorant and the vices of the learned, by the vio-
lence of mobs and the whirlwinds of war, by every hope
and every fear, by every cruelty and every crime, and by
all there is of the wild beast in the heart of man.

The discussion of such an important topic must have been
of a very interesting character, Mr. Gladstone being the
first politician and divine this country can produce; whilst

Colonel Ingersoll is held to be the first orator of the great
American Republic. Of Mr. Gladstone's eminent abilities
we are all cognizant, and it is pleasant to notice that
he had the good grace and candour to admit that his
opponent the Colonel "writes with a rare and enviable
brilliancy." It appears quite evident, judging from a
rational and secular point of view, that Jesus Christ has
utterly failed, not only in his mission first indicated—that
of becoming King of Israel—but he also failed in the
mission which his disciples imagined for him after his
death, viz., that he came down to this world to procure
the salvation of mankind. Now if mankind, according to
Christian doctrine, has fallen into a lost condition, have
they recovered from that unhappy state by and through
Christ, in conjunction with all the apparatus put in force
for the propagation of Christianity? The answer is to be
found in the fact that to-day the vast bulk of the human
race are non-Christian, and ever likely to be, and to all
these the glad tidings of the Gospel (so-called) are nothing
less than the tidings of eternal damnation. Had not
Jesus power to save these millions? I can see but one
excuse that it is not done, viz., his inability. Depraved as
mankind do seem, and brutal as many really are, the
monster, I presume, was never born that would leave
untold millions of sensitive beings to endure eternal tor-
ment if he could possibly prevent it. And if Jesus Christ
possesses the illimitable power attributed to him, it is
sheer imbecility to say that he could not prevent it if he
would. The case, then, stands thus: Christ could convert
the different peoples of the earth to the Christian faith
with alacrity and in a short period of time, were he disposed so to do. But as this achievement has not taken
place, we are driven to the conclusion that his mission to
the world, as defined by his disciples, has wholly failed,
and that consequently the Christian system has collapsed.
But, alas, upon the foundation of the life and death of
Christ and the doctrines taught by his followers has arisen
a system of religion of a most arbitrary, inequitable, and
irrational character. It appears to have been originated
by Peter, Christ's chief lieutenant, an ardent and most
energetic apostle, some time after the death of Christ. This
was the apostle who emphatically stated that Jesus was
the Christ, the son of the living God, and afterwards in
his presence denied with oaths any knowledge of him.

Peter was the chief who appears to have laid the foundation for the compulsory support of religion. Nearly the first of his assumed miracles was to strike dead two generous-hearted people because they did not part with the whole amount their property was sold for, and lay it all at the apostles' feet. One would have thought that the apostles would have been thankful for a share of the money realised by the sale of the property, and permitted the donors to reserve a little for themselves, should they stand in need of it. But no, Peter must have it all, to put in his capacious bag. Now as to this miracle, what a moral example it was to set before the world! As evil examples are very contagious, it is by no means a matter of surprise that the spirit displayed in the initiation of the Christian faith should so thoroughly imbue the future development of the system, so that it grew with its growth. Hence we find in the present day that the Christian system, wherever it possesses power, acts in a despotic manner over mankind. Notably among other sections stands out the Church of England as a system of mental despotism and usurpation, even the Church authorities themselves appointing as teachers of religion men whom congregations are oftentimes quite averse to, and yet they are bound, by Christian or Church made law, to maintain such men through life, however incompetent, inefficient, or worthless they may be. If the case with regard to Church people is so grievous and so opposed to religious equity, what must be the feelings engendered in the minds of Nonconformists generally who are financially bound to support the Church, although they take no interest in it whatever? Is such a system adapted to create peace on earth and goodwill among men? The reverse is quite inevitable. The hardship and grievance is still much greater in the case of Wales, where the Nonconformists are in a large majority over Churchmen. But men stick to their sect and party in defiance of moral principle, or what is equitable and right, when money is a principal factor in the game. The vast revenues of the Church of England are quite sufficient to corrupt and demoralise, more or less, the best of men. What, then, must be its effect upon men of low moral qualities, but to prompt them to enter the Church for the sake of worldly gain, and thereby largely contribute to the moral retrogression of society? This vast revenue handed over by the State, consisting of many millions per year, to keep the Established Church going, is not only a great injustice to all Nonconformists, but it is derogatory to the moral and social elevation of society at large. There is no institution in the country bearing the name of religion that furnishes so many facilities, temptations, and encouragements to play the hypocrite, as does the Church of England. It would require a person with superhuman skill to invent a system better calculated to produce and foster a course of dissimulation. Yes, it is religion, not morality, that the Church of England upholds. Morality must take the back seat, Church religion pushes to the front. It is remarkably respectable. What is morality compared with it? It dwindles into comparative insignificance, and is virtually ignored. What are truth, justice, honour, equity, probity, and consistency of character, compared to conformity to the ceremonies of the Church, in the eyes of Church zealots? It is quite patent also that human nature, amongst the most favourably constituted, is not endowed with such moral power as successfully to resist temptations, especially under the influence of the rich and influential whose desire, it is quite obvious, is to maintain religious ascendancy over other denominations at any price.

After having taken a thoughtful view of religion and its diversified (and to me) incongruous doctrines, according as my abilities and opportunities permitted, I felt at length compelled, in opposition to my previous hopes and expectations, to withdraw my support from the maintenance of those views I had adopted, and cherished, as the most valuable acquirements of life. This episode in my life cost me much. It costs something in the present day of advanced Freethought, but it cost far more fifty years ago. Then Freethought was but an urchin struggling into existence, but is now encouraged and strengthened by the growing intelligence of the age and the salubrity of the atmosphere in which he moves, and promises that ere long he will become a very stalwart fellow, who will turn his back upon no man. The withdrawal from the Congregational Church was to me personally a bitter experience, intensified in consequence of the general good feeling which prevailed between myself and the most sincerely pious and consistent members of our church; and this feeling I am fully persuaded was reciprocated in a high degree on their side. But what honest course was open to me under the circumstances? I could remain in the Church only as an hypocrite. But hypocrisy stood very low in my estimation, notwithstanding its great prevalence in connection with religion. Some of my best friends warned me that, if I left the cause of religion, that respect for me would grow considerably less. This was a very unpleasant announcement to me, as I felt great pleasure in gaining and retaining the good opinion of my friends of all denominations ; but unfortunately this announcement proved true, and I began to realise the import of that passage of Scripture where Jesus said : "I came not to send peace, but a sword." And again : " For I am come to set a man at variance against his father, and the daughter against her mother, and the daughter-in-law against her mother-in-law. And a man's foes shall be those of his own household."

I cannot think that the sentiments here expressed have a tendency to confirm our ideas that Jesus is really the Prince of Peace. We find unfortunately in the present day that this spirit of persecution has not died out, this sword still remains unsheathed, although its edge has become much more blunt than it was in the days of yore. But I conclude from experience that whatever we suffer in the way of persecution with regard to religion, there remains a satisfactory and pleasurable feeling that we are honest enough and loyal enough to the interests of truth, to stand firmly by our strongest and most reasonable convictions, in the face of the frowns of the hoary-headed dame, Mrs. Grundy. Having accompanied my Christian friends far on their Christian pilgrimage, we arrived at the " Parting of the Ways," when the severance took place, they continuing to travel on the " Great Substitutionary" or sentimental line, which they did with apparent pleasure and self-complacency. For my own part I felt unable to accompany them any further upon this line, as I became firmly convinced that, in order to travel thereon with equanimity of mind, I should have to suppress or ignore my earnest convictions. This appeared to me an inconsistent and incongruous course for a rational and moral being to pursue. Consequently I left my friends with much regret and took another line, that of " Ethical Progress," which runs from the capital Superstition, through the vale of Ignorance and Vice, to the beautiful "City of

Morality," situate on the hill of Rational Enjoyment.   In
this city all are equally eligible that can endorse the
aphorism—"There is no religion higher than truth."
Here people of every creed and clime who adopt a rational
policy in life receive a cordial welcome.   Here alone are
those that repudiate class interests, and throw overboard
caste privileges, and look upon mankind as one universal
brotherhood.   Here the philosopher, the scientist, the
philanthropist, the Theosophist, the Universalist, and all
others who attempt to elucidate truth, promote morality,
and endeavour to unfold the secrets of nature, may work
in accord with each other.   Here there is no class nor
hereditary privilege, no honours but what spring from
personal merit or ability.   Here men are not valued by
their wealth or the antiquity of their pedigree, but by
their usefulness in the service of mankind.

A RETROSPECT,

AND ADVICE TO TOILERS.

I now take a glance at some important incidents of my
life hitherto unnoticed.   I can just remember the great
agitation relative to the unhappy disagreement between
George IV and his wife, Queen Caroline.   My maternal
uncle, with whom I then lived, took interest in the matter,
he being in favour of the Queen.   This would be about
the year 1819.   But up to the year 1830, I knew little of
politics, when the great Reform Bill controversy woke me
up.   At that time the people were unrepresented in
Parliament.   Farmers, tradesmen, men of property or
no property, were equally voteless.   Clergymen and
landed proprietors only had this privilege.   By this Bill,
£50 renters were enfranchised.   The Tories, as usual when
any political power is given to the people, strongly
protested, avowing that if the Bill was carried it would
be the ruin of the country.   But it was neither its ruin,
nor much to its advantage, except as an initiation, or a
preliminary step to greater reforms.   For without the

ballot as a protection to voters in dependent circumstances, the use or extension of the franchise among the people is of little avail. The ambition and conceit of human nature is so great, that the aristocracy strongly opposes the carrying out the principles of political equity towards those in a subordinate position. The Tory school of politics is a channel in which this spirit finds a free development, as I have abundantly proved by noting the conduct of the Tory party from the passing of the great Reform Bill (socalled) to the present day.

The Liberals for about thirty years endeavoured to pass the Ballot Act to protect the dependent voter from the intimidating action of despotic landlords and employers of working men. Why were the Liberals opposed when attempting to carry into law such an equitable act of legislation? There was but one cause, viz., despots were afraid that dependent voters might have a will of their own, and as men of principle might carry it out agreeably to the interests of their own class. The Tories condemned the Ballot Act as an un-English legislation. Yes, unhappily it was too well described. It has been more in accordance with English practice to coerce and overrule the convictions of those who were found in a subordinate condition of life.

About the year 1840 a Charter was drawn up favourable to the political interests of the working-classes, which was so opposed by those in power that it well nigh produced a revolution. But how stands the matter to-day respecting this Charter? Well, nearly every point thereof has become law, despite the persistent opposition of the Tories to every measure of reform in the interests of those doing the drudgery of life.

In the year 1838, through the imposition of the Corn Laws, the wheat had risen to seventy-seven shillings per quarter, whilst the labourers received the magnificent wages of seven to nine shillings per week. The Liberals, therefore, under the inspiration of Messrs. Cobden and Bright, had to labor for years, subject to calumny and danger, in order to abolish this abominable impost, created for the purpose of enriching the landlords at the cost of the labouring part of the community. Since then the labouring population have fared much better than they did previously. They are better fed, clothed, and educated. And whom have they to thank for it? The Liberals, who have laboured to obtain laws in their favour, or the Tories who have persistently opposed every measure calculated to procure them advantage? No working-man possessed of common-sense would voluntarily vote for a Tory Parliamentary candidate, save through sheer political ignorance.

In 1852, when 37 years old, occurred the most important transaction of my life. In that year I was fortunate enough to secure a help-mate possessed of qualities adapted to make a comfortable home, and cheer the path of life by her judicious counsel and incessant attention to matters of both trivial and serious importance, calculated to procure peace and concord, which we have enjoyed in no small degree for a period of over forty-two years. Notwithstanding some serious drawbacks for which neither of us are in the slightest degree responsible, we can yet look back upon these years of happiness with great pleasure and complacency, although some of our friends predicted that our union would be an unhappy one, in consequence of want of unanimity in religious ideas. But happily these predictions were wholly falsified by the exercise of a broad charity, which harbours no bigotry, or unfriendliness for diversity of opinion. And I may further add that, amongst our six children, the eldest of whom has reached the age of forty and the youngest twenty years and upwards, there has not been one undistinguished for general honesty and veracity of character. This, I maintain, is presumptive proof that their home education has not been of an unsatisfactory description, and I think perhaps not often equalled; and this consciousness affords not a little gratification.

An episode of a very remarkable character that has been enacted within the last twenty years I cannot pass without referring to. It is the treatment that was meted out to Charles Bradlaugh, M.P., by our legislature, prompted by the religious zeal and bigotry of the country, especially as represented by the Church of England. Here was a man that made a life sacrifice in favour of the poorer classes,—a man possessed of extraordinary physical, mental, and moral powers, which he devoted in the most unselfish form to the cause of the working classes, and who, through his exceptional abilities and habits of persistent industry, ascended from the depths of poverty to the honourable position of that of a member of Parliament for this kingdom of Great Britain. Although still a poor man, he was one of the most honest men that ever put his foot in Parliament, and as a poor man's representative he has no equal yet, although we have at present the best People's Parliament ever elected in this country. It is now a matter of history how he was treated by the British Christian public; how he was prevented occupying his seat after being duly elected time after time; how he was also dragged out of Parliament by physical force to his great personal injury. All this was the result of religious zeal for the cause of God. In this way our Christian zealots recommended Christianity to the people by virtually putting to death, by a kind of inch to inch process, over a series of years, a man of rare and enviable ability and high moral character. Yes, this inhuman and brutal conduct, the effect of Christian zeal, must go down in history to future time with its indelible stain, which no process can ever eradicate.

In concluding this my Autobiography, I beg to offer my brother farmers a word of advice arising from a long life of experience only, without assuming for a moment any other claim to make such a proposition beyond my respect for them, and desire for their general welfare; for as a class I consider them second to none in honesty, industry, and loyalty to their convictions. But they are unfortunately in an unfavourable position to ascertain the right or wrong of the different religious teachings imposed upon mankind. How are farmers, and others as unfavourably situated, to deal with these matters? Are they credulously to receive these contradictory teachings as the word or inspiration of God? If so, then they may imbibe Muhammadanism, Mormonism, Buddhism, Theosophy, or any of the doctrines taught by the very numerous divergent sections of Christianity. But men should not forget that they are possessed of reasoning powers which they should not ignore or renounce, to follow the dictates of others whose education may be extensive, and whose eloquence may be considerable, inasmuch as men of the greatest learning and general ability differ with regard to religious opinions, as broadly as the most uneducated people. My humble advice, therefore, is: That every man possessed of common-sense would do well to use his own judgment upon all public questions, which it is quite certain the bulk of men do not, or they would not retain the views in manhood imposed upon them in infancy, before their reasoning powers were at all developed. We know full well that each different system of religion cannot be true, and, as it is a matter of great importance, every person should do his best to fathom it out, so far as his judgment and opportunity permit. But this is not to be attained by listening demurely and credulously to the preaching of those in whose opinions you may even place considerable confidence. The bull should be taken by the horns. You must submit every difficult question to the arbitration of reason; if it can pass that bar, respect it as pure gold. If it fail to pass there, reject it as a spurious article that should be thrown under the foot of man, no matter what its popularity or how remote the antiquity of its origin. Doctrines that are not in accordance with humane sentiments and reasonable convictions should be discarded as unworthy the reception of individuals aspiring to the attainment of moral culture. Nevertheless, every doctrine should be tested dispassionately and deliberately before it is finally accepted or rejected. Especially should we weigh carefully, and judge impartially, the opinions of those whose views are opposed to our own. There are dreadful doctrines taught, calculated to bewilder and overturn the equilibrium of the greatest mental power were they fully believed in, which happily they are not, even by the greatest professors, without a considerable sprinkling of *salt*, or, in other words, *the pure mercy of God*, arising from a consciousness of the merciful feelings that inhabits the human breast. But it is a cruel, a terrible thing to impose the doctrine of eternal damnation upon the minds of tender, sensitive beings, year after year and century after century. This monstrous doctrine engenders consternation and terror in timid, nervous individuals at the approach of death. There is also another important consideration that must not be overlooked. That is, the vast amount of money yearly squandered to keep this diabolical doctrine afloat. Millions of pounds per annum, that should be used for the requirements and comforts of the working classes, pass into the hands of the wealthy and others, who live only as birds of prey upon the industry of the farmers and the laboring classes of the community. How long will men of good understanding submit in this age of progress to all the imposition and delusion that are practised upon society, to the great disadvantage of those that comprise the middle and lower classes thereof? My final advice to my brother farmers is to look well to their class interests. If they fail to do this, I am unable to see what claim they have to be considered either patriots or philanthropists. With regard to the upper classes, they are quite capable of taking care of themselves without our interference. But I think it right and proper to accord to them the honour and respect of which they are worthy, appraising them not by the vastness of their wealth, but by their intellectual and moral qualities, and the value of their services to mankind generally. Yet I hold that it is a great mistake to suppose that the lower class of society would be one whit better than the upper class, were it possible thoroughly to reverse their circumstances. They would require quite as much looking after, would be equally as ambitious, overbearing, and inequitably disposed to those in a subordinate position of life as are the rich and influential of to-day. Human nature is similar throughout society. There are excellent natural qualities in men of all classes and of all political and religious persuasions, and the full development of these qualities should be considered as the most important and beneficial object within the province of man.

I hope to be pardoned for offering a word of advice here to young men, agriculturists and others. I think it would show good sense and self-control in them to develope their own abilities, physically, mentally, and morally. If munificently gifted by the beneficence of nature, how sad and culpable must it be to neglect the cultivation of such minds; and if, unfortunately, the mind is of an inferior quality, the more reason that its possessor should cultivate it to its utmost extent to enable him to cope efficiently with his fellows. There are various reasons, of much importance, why the intellect should receive all possible culture.. Now the attainment of truth and the reception of correct ideas is not to be secured without earnest and persistent effort to obtain truth for truth's sake. Difficulties may arise with regard to many topics, but don't be disconcerted on that account; apply your mind to them again and again, until you obtain a satisfactory conclusion, which in all probability you will, if the difficulty is solvable by the human understanding; but, if not, you need not trouble about it. There is much more beyond the power of our comprehension than within its domain. Right and wrong, truth and falsehood, are in perpetual antagonism with each other. But it should be our object and duty as moral and rational beings to distinguish between them and to embrace the good and reject the evil. It appears to me that mankind are in nothing more beguiled and befooled than by religious ideas. Priestcraft of some kind or other, in every country, and in every age, has managed to victimise the common people by the assumption of superior knowledge relative to another life, and by playing upon the hopes and fears and sentimental feelings of the industrious part of mankind, in whose ignorance and ductility consists the web of their strength. But what does any clergy really know relative to anything beyond the precincts of the present life? Nothing whatever. The Archbishop of Canterbury and the most learned divines know no more respecting any hereafter than the most illiterate of the human species, although he (the Archbishop) draws by his pretensions £15,000 per year from the country. The hewers of wood and drawers of water, those that spin and toil, should exercise their brains more upon such important subjects, and bring all creeds and theories to the test of reason without fear. You need fear nothing but wrong-doing. But remember it is wrong to abstain from right-doing. The various priesthoods, with a view to keep the people in subjection to their craft, dwell upon the influence of supernatural beings, affirming their malevolent power over mankind. This specious theory they have wielded to their own worldly advantage and the subjugation of the people. Believe them not. Nor fear all the devils that have ever taken possession of the imagination of the most fertile and superstitious brains. But some may contend that they are so much absorbed in business to procure a living, that they have not time and opportunity to attend to these important matters. But the gravity and importance of these topics should induce you to give your best thought and judgment to the examination of them. You do not allow strangers to intermeddle with your money or other valuables. Then why depute to, or allow others, to decide for you important doctrines of a disputed and widely controversial character.

The want of time is the excuse generally given as a justification to cover our delinquencies. But we are apt to overlook the vast amount of precious time wasted in smoking, drinking and in following sports of different kinds such as football and cricket—sports quite unnecessary and even harmful for those connected with farming business. The industrious agriculturist finds in the pursuit of his calling quite as much use for the activity of his muscles as is beneficial to him, and sometimes to his hurt, and he cannot follow these athletic sports much without suffering in a business point of view. Another kind of sport injurious in many ways to the farmer is fox-hunting. That it is an exciting sport is admitted, but unless a farmer has some independency he had better abstain from it altogether. I have known farmers, even in a superior condition of life, brought to grief by following the hounds. They with their families have in consequence had to descend into the depths of poverty. Some think that by putting in an appearance in the hunting field they secure the good-will of the gentry. They may procure a smile— as the presence of the farmer serves as a cover for the intrusion of the gentry. But landlords uniformly admire the man that sticks to his farm far before him that takes pride in frequently shouting out " Tally Ho" in the hunt.

Now there is one day in the week called the Sabbath day, when labour is generally suspended by law. This I regard as a favourable opportunity for people generally to improve their minds. Some spend much of their time in attending places of worship, without, as I think, obtaining any corresponding improvement; and, were it not that they obtain information from other sources, they would be no further advanced to-day than a year ago. But I think that people having any desire to cultivate their mental powers should carefully secure their Sunday leisure for that important purpose, and they should endeavour to obtain the best publications within their reach, whether books or periodicals, for without these there is no progress. To obtain the opinion of the best, the most competent men on every side, should be our earnest desire. The ascertaining of the truth, the whole truth and nothing but the truth, upon all the important matters that present themselves to our understanding, should be our chief object. We should buy the truth, cost what it may, and when obtained prize it as gold, yea, as much fine gold. But this is not always obtained without some adverse consequences. You may be sincere, earnest, truth-loving, conscientious, and moral in conduct, but if you take a road of your own, you may find friends whom you highly value on account of their amiable characteristics, turn their backs upon you because you cannot see as they see, nor walk the path they choose to adopt. And you may also find to your dismay that, notwithstanding the eulogistic description of charity given by St. Paul in his epistles to the Corinthians, that there is nothing more scarce in the religious world than true charity. Bigotry you may commonly find in the height of her arrogance, lifting her egotistic, haughty, Pharisaic brow, and whispering audibly, "I thank my God that I am not as other men." Now, according to the declaration of St. Paul, he holds charity up as a test question of religious sincerity. He ignores all other virtues in the absence of true charity. "Without charity," he says, "I am nothing." If we are to accept this dictum of the apostle as a fact, what a number of Nothingarians is Christian society composed of to-day! Personally, I should never select the Church as the home, or depository of charity, having experienced much greater liberality of thought outside, than within its precincts. To those in the earnest pursuit of truth, I would say that, whatever uncharitableness and unpleasantness you may meet with in the pursuit of such a commendable and honourable course, you will have the satisfaction and gratification of having used your judgment honestly and conscientiously, which cannot fail to secure that peace of mind which the world cannot give nor take away.

I now close this my humble Autobiography, leaving it, with all its imperfections, as my legacy to the industrious classes of the community, and as the only compensation I can render for the advantages, privileges, and comforts I have received therefrom. In wishing well to all classes of society, I desire that the industrious portion thereof should make greater progress in moral and material well-being, and that they should stand firmly by the principles of truth, justice, and equity, as their only security against error, despotism, and oppression.

A. BONNER, Printer, 34 Bouverie Street, London, E.C.